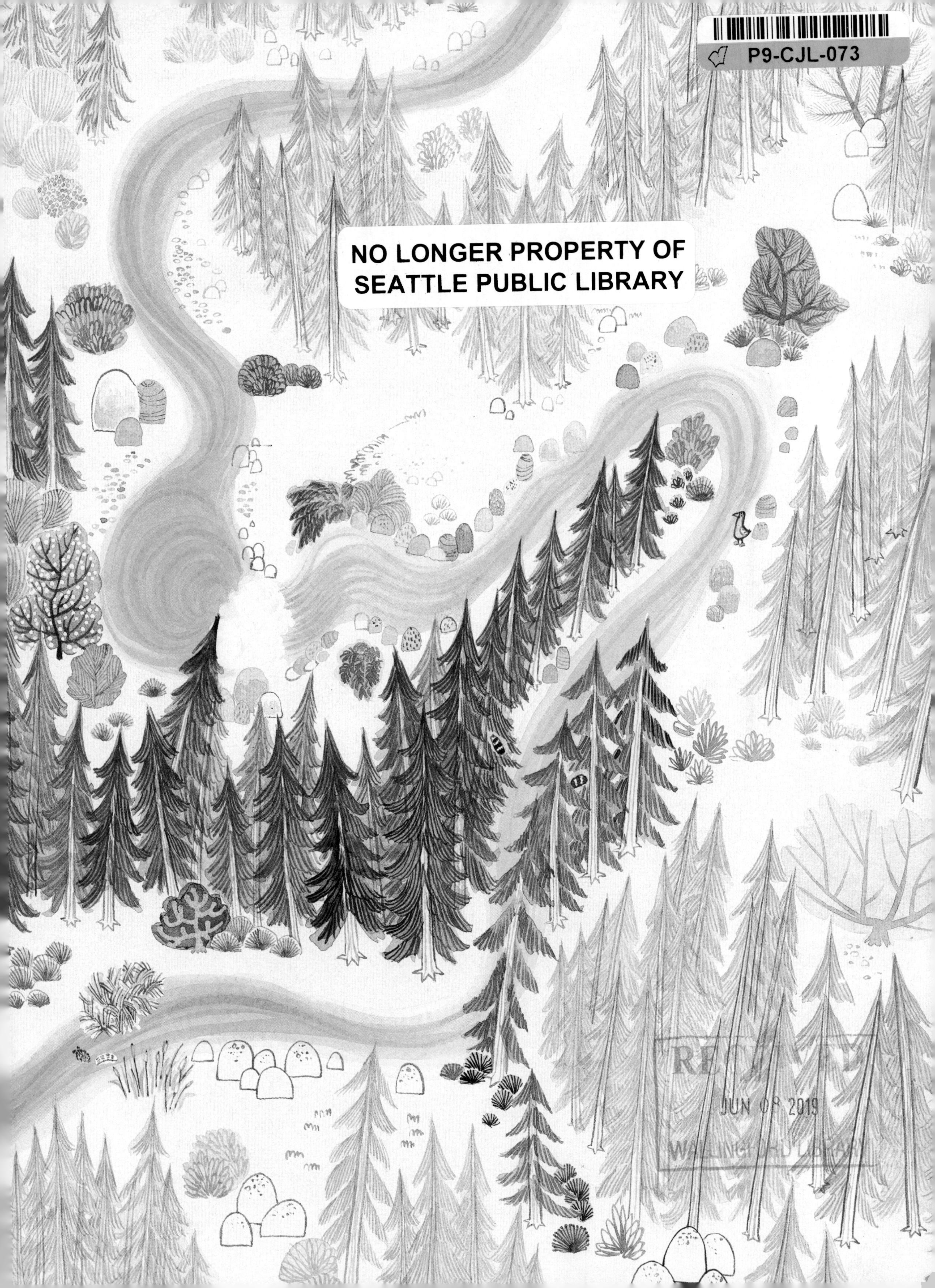

BEAR CAME ALONG

by Richard T. Morris

Illustrated by
LeUyen Pham

LB

LITTLE, BROWN AND COMPANY
NEW YORK   BOSTON

Once there was a river
that flowed night and day,

but it didn't know
it was a river...

until...

Bear came along.

Bear was just being curious...

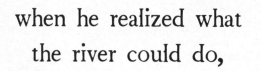

when he realized what
the river could do,

but he didn't know
he was on an
adventure...

until...

Froggy hopped on.

Froggy was a lonely frog who was looking for a friend,

but she didn't know how many she had...

until...

The Turtles tried to warn them about the things that could go wrong,

the Turtles showed up.

but they didn't know how to enjoy the ride...

until...

Beaver climbed aboard.

Beaver was
born to captain;
he knew exactly
where to go,

but he didn't know
about the detours

until ...

the Raccoons dropped in.

The Raccoons were so excited

about the twists and turns ahead,

but they didn't know they had to be careful...

until...

they crashed into Duck.

Duck was so content being right where she was,
but she didn't know there was a world to see...

until...

Bear held on to Froggy!

Froggy held on to Turtles!

Turtles held on to Beaver!

Beaver held on to Raccoons!

Raccoons held on to Duck!

Oh, what a ride!

So many different animals
living their separate lives,
but they didn't know they
were in it together...

until...

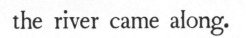

the river came along.

AUTHOR'S NOTE

If you spend too much time thinking about certain things, sometimes you get lucky and find a story. That's what happened with *Bear Came Along*. As a parent, I learned pretty quickly that kids are born with inherent personalities. We do our best to guide them, but their distinctive characteristics define who they are. All these diverse personalities go out into the world and balance one another. Sometimes the hardest thing to do is to embrace the other, especially when that other is so different. But it is through this connection that we truly discover our best selves—our strengths, our weaknesses, our fears, our courage. This story says, "Take a chance!" "Hop on board!" "Work together!" "Trust each other!" "Share the adventure!" I hope you enjoy the ride.

—Richard T. Morris

ARTIST'S NOTE

This book is really special to me. It was one of those rare stories that, the moment I read it, I knew exactly how it would look. I knew exactly who Bear was, and Froggy, and the rest of these lovable characters. And I knew that this story, which started out so simple, so black-and-white, was the perfect metaphor for life. While painting this book, I spent a lot of time thinking about why people become divided from one another and forget that they all live on the same earth. It takes a small thing, like animals in a forest falling into a river, to realize this. We sink or swim together. And sometimes we take a tumble and things turn out all right.

I've illustrated over one hundred books, and I have to admit it's hard to find the right story. Just a little funny, just a little sweet, and simple in the way only a perfect truth can be. This story is, to me, exactly that. A small metaphor that reminds us that the things that bind us are greater than the things that divide us, and that while we are each distinct from one another, with quirks that make us so unique, we're all journeying down the same river together. It's so easy to forget that sometimes. But every once in a while, a story comes along that gets it just right.

—LeUyen Pham

For my parents —RTM

For Alex, Leo, and Adrien —LP

ABOUT THIS BOOK The illustrations for this book were done in watercolor, ink, and gouache on hot-press illustration board. This book was edited by Alvina Ling and designed by Jamie W. Yee with art direction by Saho Fujii. The production was supervised by Erika Schwartz, and the production editor was Jen Graham. The text was set in 1790 Royal Printing, and the display type was hand-lettered.